WALT DISNEY'S
BUNNY BOOK

TOLD BY JANE WERNER

ILLUSTRATIONS BY THE WALT DISNEY STUDIO

ADAPTED BY DICK KELSEY AND BILL JUSTICE

gb®

A GOLDEN PRESS BOOK

Western Publishing Company, Inc.

New York, New York • Racine, Wisconsin

GOLDEN, A BIG GOLDEN BOOK, and GOLDEN PRESS ®
are trademarks of Western Publishing Company, Inc.

THIS BIG GOLDEN BOOK WAS PRODUCED UNDER THE SUPERVISION OF
THE WALT DISNEY STUDIO

Deep in the woods, where the brier bushes
grow, lies Bunnyville, a busy little bunny-
rabbit town.

And in the very center of that busy little town stands a cottage—a neat twig cottage with a neat brown roof—which is known to all as Great-Grandpa Bunny Bunny's very own home.

Great-Grandpa Bunny Bunny, as every bunny knows, was the ancestral founder of the town, which is, as everyone knows, a very fine thing to be.

Great-Grandpa Bunny Bunny knew many wonderful stories.

He liked to tell the young bunnies who gathered round how he and Mrs. Bunny Bunny, when they were very young, had found that very brier patch and had built themselves that very same little twig house.

It was a happy life they lived there, deep in the woods, bringing up their bunny family in that little house of twigs.

And, of course, Daddy Bunny Bunny, as he was called then, was busy at his job, decorating Easter eggs.

As the children grew up, they helped to paint Easter eggs. Soon they were all grown-up, with families of their own, and they built a ring of their own houses all around their parents' home.

By and by they had a town there, and they called it Bunnyville.

Now Grandpa Bunny Bunny had lots of help painting Easter eggs—so much that he began to look for other jobs to do.

He taught some of the young folks to paint
the flowers in the woods.

They tried out some new shades of green
on mosses and ferns.

They made the woods so beautiful that People who went walking there marveled at the colors as they talked among themselves.

"The soil must be especially rich," they said, "or the rainfall especially wet."

And the bunnies would hear them and silently laugh, for they knew it was all Grandpa Bunny Bunny's doing.

Years went by. Now there were still more families in Bunnyville. And Grandpa Bunny Bunny had finally grown to be Great-Grandpa Bunny Bunny, for that is how things go. He still supervised all the Easter-egg painting, and he watched over the work on the flowers every spring.

But now he had *so* much help that between times he looked for other jobs to do.

He taught some of the bunnies to paint the autumn leaves—purple for the gum trees, yellow for the elms, patterns in scarlet for the sugar maple trees. Through the woods they scampered with their brushes and their pails of paint.

And the People who went walking there would say among themselves, "Never has there been such color in these woods. The fall nights must have been especially frosty hereabouts."

And the bunnies would hear them and silently laugh, for they knew it was all their great-grandpa's plan.

And so it went as the seasons rolled round.
Each season saw more and more bunnies in
that busy Bunnyville.

And Great-Grandpa was busy finding jobs
for them to do.

He taught them in winter to paint shadows
on the snow . . .

and to draw pictures in frost on wintry
windowpanes and to polish up the diamond
lights on glittering icicles.

Between times he told stories to each crop of bunny youngsters, round the cozy fire in his neat little twig home. The bunny children loved Great-Grandpa and his funny bunny tales, and they loved the new and different things he found for them to do.

But at last it did seem as if he'd thought of everything! He even had crews of bunnies trained to paint the first tiny buds of spring.

He had teams who waited beside cocoons, to touch up the wings of new butterflies.

Others specialized in beetles, still others in creeping, crawling things.

They had painted up that whole wildwood till it sparkled and it gleamed.

And now, the bunnies wondered, what would he think of next? Well, Great-Grandpa stayed at home a lot those days, and he thought and thought and thought.

And at last he told a secret to that season's bunny boys and girls.

"Children," Great-Grandpa Bunny Bunny said, "I am going away. And I'll tell you what my next job will be, if you'll promise not to say a word about it."

So the bunny children promised, and Great-Grandpa went away. The older bunnies missed him, and often they looked sad. But the bunny children only smiled and looked extremely wise, for they knew a secret they had promised not to tell.

Then one day a windy rainstorm pelted down on Bunnyville. Everyone scampered speedily home and stayed cozy and dry in his house.

After a while the rain slowed down to single dripping drops.

Then every front door opened, and out the bunny children ran.

"Oh, it's true!" those bunnies shouted, and they did a bunny dance. "Great-Grandpa's been at work again. Come see what he has done this time!"

And the People walking out that day looked up in pleased surprise.

"Have you ever," they cried, "simply *ever* seen a sunset so gorgeously bright?"

The little bunnies heard them, and they chuckled silently, for they knew that it was all Great-Grandpa Bunny Bunny's plan.